BUT i READ iT ON THE iNTERNET!

Toni Buzzeo

Illustrations by
Sachiko Yoshikawa

UpstartBooks

Madison, Wisconsin
www.upstartbooks.com

*To Jim Charette and the fabulous
staff at Burbank Branch Library,
without whom I would be aimlessly
adrift in a sea of books.
—T. B.*

*For my uncle, Yasuyuki Miyazaki.
—S. Y.*

Published by UpstartBooks
4810 Forest Run Road
Madison, WI 53704
1-608-241-1201

Text © 2013 by Toni Buzzeo
Illustrations © 2013 by Sachiko Yoshikawa

PRESIDENTS

The first thing I noticed when I walked into class on Monday morning was the bulletin board. I grinned. Who did Mr. Dickinson rope into making all those flags?

Just then, my librarian, Mrs. Skorupski, sailed in. I checked her accessories. Yep, she was definitely in on this.

She dumped an armful of books on Mr. Dickinson's chair.

"What's up with the flags?" I asked.

"Oh, this research project is custom-made for a fact-meister like you, Hunter!"

Before I could say, "Fact-meister?" Carmen Rosa Peña tripped through the door and dropped her half-eaten granola bar on the floor. She scooped it up and took another bite.

"Ewwww, disgusting!" I said.

"Five-second rule, Hunter Harris. It takes five seconds for bacterial contamination."

"Says who?"

Carmen popped the last bite in her mouth. "Says the *Internet!*"

"Oh, brother," I muttered. Carmen and her infallible Internet!

After roll call, Mr. Dickinson dug right in. He flashed a K-W-L chart on the whiteboard. "Who KNOWS something interesting about a U.S. president?"

"Abraham Lincoln was the tallest!"

"Kennedy was the youngest elected!"

"One president was born on the fourth of July!"

Mr. Dickinson typed as fast as he could.

Then Carmen's voice cut through all the others. "George Washington had wooden teeth!"

"No, he didn't," I said.

"Yes, he did," she insisted.

KNOW	WANT TO KNOW	LEARNED

"Hunter and Carmen," Mr. Dickinson said. "You seem to have different opinions. Let's start with the source of your information."

"I read a biography about Washington—a *true book*," I said.

Carmen threw me a withering look. "But I read it on the *Internet*."

Mr. Dickinson grabbed his laptop. "Follow me, class!"

KNOW	WANT TO KNOW	LEARN
Lincoln was the tallest.		
Kennedy was youngest elected.		
...esident was born July 4.		
...hington had wooden teet...		
...was named after Theodore...		
...Jefferson invented macaroni and cheese.		
...ohn Quincy Adams had a pet alligator at the White House.		
...drew Johnson never attended school.		

In the library, Mrs. Skorupski projected our chart. "Okily dokily. Who wants to challenge anything in the KNOW column?"

I raised my hand.

"Hunter is challenging Washington's wooden teeth. We'll highlight it in red and try to verify it," Mr. Dickinson said.

Carmen threw a just-you-wait look my way.

"I don't think a stuffed animal would actually be named for a president," Patty said.

"What if the president was Theodore Roosevelt and his nickname was Teddy?" I asked.

"Oh," Patty said. "Maybe it *was* named for him then."

"So let's highlight it in yellow—meaning we'll proceed with caution," said Mrs. Skorupski.

When we finished highlighting, Carmen announced, "I made a list of all those highlighted items. I'll check the Internet and bring in the facts tomorrow."

The Internet, the Internet! Gram and I might not have the Internet. We might not even have a computer. But I knew lots more true facts than Carmen—all from books.

"That's very generous of you, Carmen," Mr. Dickinson said. "But actually…"

I held my breath. *Finally*, I thought, *he's going to set her straight about the Internet.*

"…Mrs. Skorupski and I have a different plan."

Before I could exhale, Mr. Dickinson added more "facts" to our K-W-L chart—"to increase the challenge," he said.

"For homework, choose one red item, one yellow item, and one un-highlighted item," said Mrs. Skorupski. "Verify that each one is true—or not true. And let Mr. Dickinson know where you found the information. That's called citing your sources."

"If you use sources from the Internet," added Mr. Dickinson, "cite them by giving me the URLs."

I stayed behind and checked out another Washington biography, plus one about Theodore Roosevelt. Books! The best place to find *true* facts.

The next morning, we met Mrs. Skorupski in the multipurpose room to share our results.

"The teddy bear *was* named after President Theodore Roosevelt," Hugh Abernathy said.

"How did you verify it?" Mr. Dickinson asked.

His twin, Louis, plopped a bear on the table. "Carmen's sister, Frieda, helped us. Her teddy bear has a tag that says so."

Mr. Dickinson tapped the tag. "Do we all agree that this is a reliable source?"

"My grandma bought that bear for my sister at the Smithsonian Museum," Carmen said. "The *Smithsonian*!"

Robert raised his hand. "But the Smithsonian didn't make the bear. And companies will say anything about their stuff to make you buy it."

"Well...," I paused. I really hated to admit this. "I think Carmen's right, because I read it in a biography of Roosevelt."

"So if it's in a book, it's true?" Mrs. Skorupski asked.

"Maybe not always," I said. "But the author is a professor. And the publisher publishes a lot of nonfiction books for kids. And you had it in the library collection. I know you buy only books with *true* facts!"

"Excellent evaluation of your source, Hunter," she said.

"Besides," said Carmen, "*I* read it on the Internet!"

"Okay, Carmen, let's pull up your website." Mr. Dickinson entered the URL into the location bar.

Suddenly half a dozen teddy bears dressed like famous people filled the screen, accompanied by the notes of "Teddy Bears' Picnic." Mr. Dickinson clicked on a chubby bear wearing glasses and a safari vest.

"The teddy bear was named after the twenty-sixth president of the United States," Carmen read. "Theodore Roosevelt. See?"

"That's the same as the tag on Frieda's bear," Robert said. "They're just trying to sell it!"

"But they couldn't say it if it wasn't true." Carmen's voice shook a little.

"Or maybe they could," said Mrs. Skorupski, handing us each a copy of her *Website Evaluation Gizmo*.

Mrs. Skorupski's Website Evaluation Gizmo

INFORMATIVE?

Can you read and understand the information on the website?	yes	no
Does the website have information that answers your questions?	yes	no
Do the illustrations help you to understand the information?	yes	no
Are there links to other sources you can also use?	yes	no

EASY TO USE?

Is the font easy to read, and is the layout uncrowded and simple?	yes	no
Are the headings clear?	yes	no
Can you navigate (move about) the website easily?	yes	no
Is it clear which section of the website has the information you need?	yes	no
Is the website searchable?	yes	no

ACCURATE?

Who owns the website?		
What does the URL end with (.com, .edu, .gov, etc.)? What can you tell about the website from the URL?		
Is the website owner an organization or person with knowledge on your topic?	yes	no
Is the website selling you anything?	yes	no
Has the website been updated recently?	yes	no

"Let's use the Gizmo to evaluate the ACCURACY of this website," Mrs. Skorupski said.

Robert raised his hand. "They're definitely selling us something."

I added, "The owner is Berr-y Bears. They might not know much about presidents."

"But they do know a lot about teddy bears," Carmen said.

Mr. Dickinson laughed. "That's true."

"What about the URL www.berr-ybears.com?" asked Mrs. Skorupski.

We all just looked at her.

"This URL ends in .com, which means it's a commercial business," she said. "If it ended in .edu—for education—we'd know the information came from a school, a college, or a university."

"Super accurate, right?" Patty asked.

"Hmmm," Mr. Dickinson said. "What if it's an elementary school website with information written by fourth graders?"

"Then it just depends on how smart they are about the Internet," Carmen said.

"Or which sources they used," I snapped. "Like *books*!"

Mrs. Skorupski smiled. "Or if they answered lots of questions in the Gizmo to make sure the source was a good one."

After lunch, Mrs. Skorupski gave us our final homework assignment in the library. I noticed she'd changed her accessories.

She said that books weren't always the best source for our research questions. "If we want to know the current weather in Washington, D.C., should we use a book or the Internet?"

"Internet, of course!" Carmen crowed. "Besides, sometimes we don't *have* a book with the answer, but we *do* have an Internet connection."

I wanted to say, "Sometimes we don't *have* an Internet connection." But then she would know.

"For homework, prove or disprove one presidential 'fact' using the Internet only, and evaluate your website source using the Gizmo," Mrs. Skorupski said. "Stop and see me if you need to use the computers this afternoon or tomorrow morning."

Wouldn't you know it? Carmen and I both chose George Washington's wooden teeth.

I spotted Mrs. Skorupski on bus duty after school.

"I've got Cub Scouts right now and an allergy shot tomorrow morning," I said. "So can I just use a book for the assignment?"

"No! Absolutely no books, Hunter Harris!" We both laughed. "Could your grandma drive you to the public library tonight to do some online research?"

The Abernathy twins zipped past. Hugh yelled, "The public library rocks!"

"Have you ever been there?" she asked.

I shook my head.

"I'll write your grandma a note," she said. "Ask Mr. Charette to help you. He's the librarian in the Children's Room."

Children's Room

Biography

That evening at the public library, I was nervous when Grandma pointed me to the right room and then sat down to read a magazine. But when I walked in, Mr. Charette said, "You must be Hunter. Mrs. Skorupski said you were coming."

We got right down to business. "Now, I don't know how skilled you are online, so if I tell you something you already know, just humor an old man, okay?"

I smiled. He was funny like Mrs. Skorupski, but in a quieter way—and without the accessories.

Mr. Charette said, "Let's try a student search engine first. If we need more website suggestions, we can move on to a general one."

He suggested I type "George Washington" "wooden teeth" in the search box. Lots of website suggestions popped up on the page.

"Be patient," Mr. Charette said. "This is where the Gizmo will really come in handy."

We evaluated each site until we finally had one that was informative, easy to use, and best of all, accurate. Right there on the Internet!

Together we filled out the Gizmo for the site and e-mailed the URL to Mr. Dickinson.

Then Mr. Charette shook my hand. "I hope I'll see you regularly now—to use our computers—*and* to check out our books."

Hugh and Louis

dent born on the 4th of July?

ES   NO

urce — name of website:

urce — website's URL:

Carmen and Hunter

Did George Washington have wooden teeth?

YES   NO

Best online source — name of website:

Best online source — website's URL:

The next day was the showdown.

Mrs. Skorupski had posted one sheet for each fact on the library walls.

When Carmen whispered, "I've got the final proof," I just sat quietly next to her with my Gizmo folded in my pocket, smiling like a Cheshire cat.

At last, Mrs. Skorupski called us up. Carmen zipped to the chart with a red marker in her hand, and I followed behind.

Like a game show host, Mr. Dickinson said, "And now, Carmen and Hunter, for the one million dollar prize—just kidding!—did George Washington have wooden teeth?"

Everything happened at once.

Carmen's marker flashed up to the chart.

I pushed her hand aside, snapping, "He did not!"

And Mr. Dickinson cheered, "You're absolutely right!"

I blinked. There, in front of me, was Carmen's bright red circle around NO.

"What?" I turned to Carmen. "I mean, RIGHT! What made you change your mind?"

"I read it on the Internet! But this time I knew how to make sure the Internet was right!"

Carme
Did George Washing
YES   N
Best online source – nar
Best online source – web